Pippa Goodhart

Illustrated by

Amber Cassidy

EGMONT
We bring stories to life

Book Band: Orange

First published in Great Britain 2014
by Egmont UK Ltd
The Yellow Building, 1 Nicholas Road, London W11 4AN
Text copyright © Pippa Goodhart 2014
Illustrations copyright © Amber Cassidy 2014
The author and illustrator have asserted their moral rights.
ISBN 978 1 4052 7070 0
www.egmont.co.uk
10 9 8 7 6 5 4 3 2 1
A CIP catalogue record for this title is available from the British Library.
Printed in Singapore.
57030/1

Please note: Any website addresses listed in this book are correct at the time of
going to print. However, Egmont cannot take responsibility for any third party
content or advertising. Please be aware that online content can be subject to change
and websites can contain content that is unsuitable for children. We advise that all
children are supervised when using the internet.

EGMONT LUCKY COIN

Our story began over a century ago, when seventeen-year-old
Egmont Harald Petersen found a coin in the street.

He was on his way to buy a flyswatter, a small hand-operated
printing machine that he then set up in his tiny apartment.

The coin brought him such good luck that today Egmont has
offices in over 30 countries around the world. And that lucky
coin is still kept at the company's head offices in Denmark.

The
Windy Day

The
Wet Day

The
Warm Day

For little Alice McKeown

P. G.

For everyone who helped

along the way

A. C.

The Windy Day

6

'What a windy day!' said Miss Chutney

as she hung out her washing.

Whoops! Off flew one sock, then two!

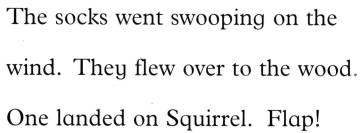

The socks went swooping on the
wind. They flew over to the wood.
One landed on Squirrel. Flap!

One landed on Mouse. Flop!

'Just what I need!' said Squirrel.

'A hat.'

'A sleeping bag to keep me warm!'

said Mouse.

The wind blew and blew, and . . .

Off flew more of Miss Chutney's

washing.

It got dark. The wind blew under
Miss Chutney's door. Wheeew!

Miss Chutney was cold without her

blanket. Shiver shiver.

But the animals
and birds were warm
under and in and on the
big tree in the wood.

13

WHEEEW! The wind blew harder.

The big tree began to creak.

Creak creak CRASH SMASH!

Mouse and Squirrel and Owl and Fox went up the hill.

16

Knock knock!

17

Soon nobody was cold
any more.

Snore!

The Wet Day

Split-splat!

It was a wet day outside and inside

Miss Chutney's house.

20

'Oh no, the roof has got a hole in it!'

said Miss Chutney.

Crash!

Some of the roof fell on to the floor.

Split-splat-splot!

'I haven't got enough money

to pay a builder to mend it!' said

Miss Chutney. 'Now I have nowhere

to live!'

'Don't worry,' said Fox. 'We will all help to get the money to pay for a new roof. You helped us, and we will help you.'

'We can sell things,' said Owl.

Fox and Squirrel took all

Miss Chutney's furniture outside.

Mouse made a sign.

Nobody wanted to buy anything.

'It is all too tatty,' said

Miss Chutney.

'Don't worry,' said Squirrel.

'We will make it all nicer.'

Mouse and Squirrel and Owl and
Fox set to work.

Soon everybody wanted to buy things. Miss Chutney had enough money to pay the builder.

There was even enough money

left over to pay for buns for tea.

The Warm Day

Miss Chutney and Mouse and Owl and Fox and Squirrel had a nice house to live in.

But it was an empty house.

What can we sit on?

'We must make new furniture,' said

Miss Chutney. 'I have an idea.

Follow me!'

Miss Chutney took some tools.

Off they went to the wood.

'We will make your old home into things for our new home,' Miss Chutney told the animals.

They all set to work again.

Fox made bowls and cups.

Miss Chutney cut logs to make a

table and stools.

The sun shone, and

Miss Chutney sang.

Saw,
saw,
Let's make
some
more!

Squirrel and Mouse wove hammocks

for beds.

Owl made a broom to sweep
the house clean.

Miss Chutney put soil into a pot.

Then she put in something else.

What
is
that?

'It's a seed. It needs soil and water and sunshine, and then it will grow into a new tree,' said Miss Chutney. 'When it is big enough, we will plant it in the wood where your old tree was.'

That made Mouse and Fox and Owl
and Squirrel and all the birds and
animals very happy.

And Miss Chutney was happy too.